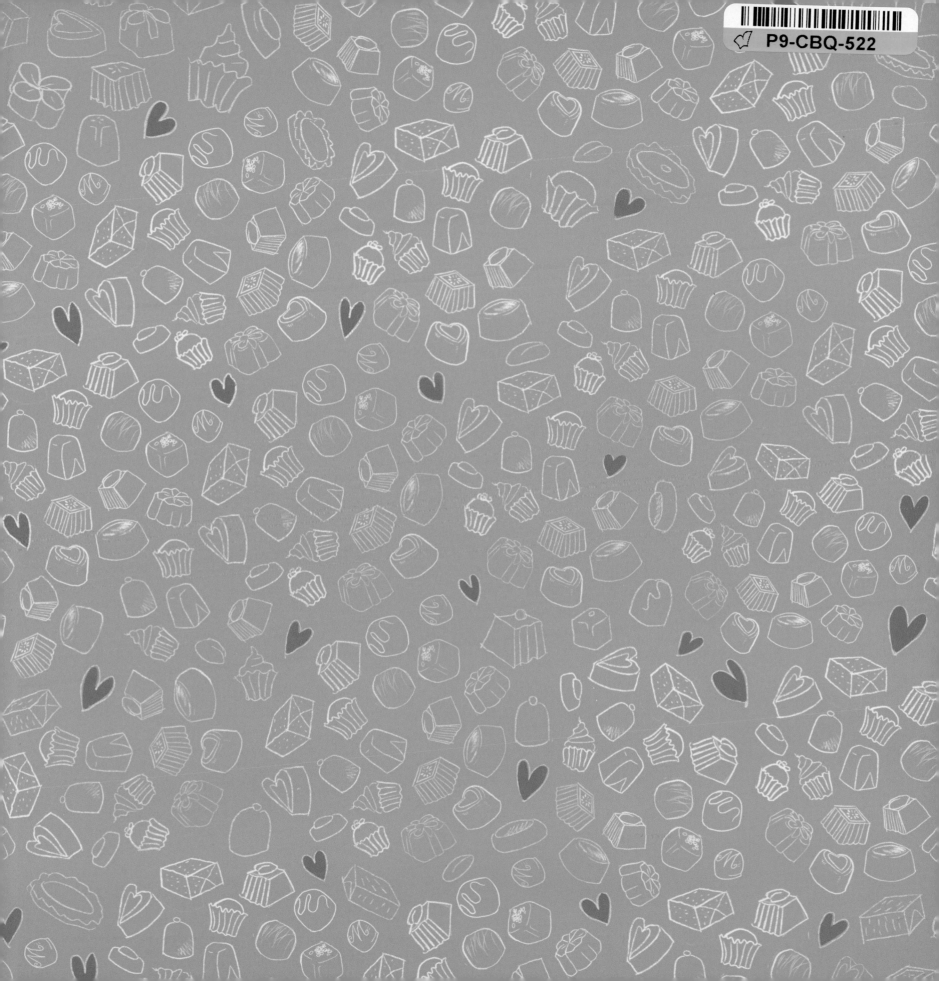

Copyright © 2022 Clavis Publishing Inc., New York

Visit us on the Web at www.clavis-publishing.com.

A Box Full of Love written by Anne Sawan and illustrated by Katrien Benaets

ISBN 978-1-60537-612-7

This book was printed in October 2021 at Nikara, M. R. Štefánika 858/25, 963 01 Krupina, Slovakia.

First Edition
10 9 8 7 6 5 4 3 2 1

Clavis Publishing supports the First Amendment and celebrates the right to read.

A Box Full of LOVE

Written by Anne Sawan
Illustrated by Katrien Benaets

Clavis
NEW YORK

Max took the top off the heart-shaped box and peeked inside.
Milk chocolate, white chocolate, dark chocolate . . .
Mama was going to love this gift!

He took a deep breath in. Mmm . . .
Maybe, he thought, *I'll try just one.*

Max licked his lips.
That last one was definitely his favorite.
Coconut covered in creamy chocolate with those
crispy, crunchy things mixed in . . . Perfect!
He couldn't wait until Mama tried them.

MAMA.

"Hi, Max," said Papa.
"What's that in your hand?"
Max let out a big sigh and shrugged his shoulders.
"It was supposed to be a Valentine's Day gift for Mama,
but I ate all the candy, so now it's nothing.
Just an empty box."
Tears filled Max's eyes.

Papa took the box and shook it.
"This box doesn't sound empty," he said. "Listen."
"I don't hear anything," said Max.

Papa opened the box. "This box is full. Look!"
"I don't see anything," said Max.

"Max," said Papa, "love isn't something you see, hear, or taste. Love is something you feel, in your heart. Love means thinking about someone and wanting to make them happy. You thought about Mama and wanted to make her happy on Valentine's Day, so you see, this box is actually full. Full of love."

Max's eyes opened wide. "It is?" he said.

"Yes," said Papa. "But if it makes you feel better,
how about we make Mama some special Valentine's Day
cookies to put inside the box along with all that love?"

"All right!" said Max.
"You get the eggs and sugar,
and I'll get the flour. Thanks, Papa."
Max ran to the kitchen and opened
the cabinet to take out the flour.
When he turned around, he noticed
a heart-shaped box, just like his,
sitting on the counter.

"Papa," asked Max, "what's that?"
"That?" said Papa, frantically mixing
the eggs and sugar together in a large bowl.
"Ahhh . . . That's another box of love for Mama."
Max smiled. "You ate all of the candy too, didn't you, Papa?"

"Yes," said Papa.
"Now hand me that flour
so we can finish these cookies
before she gets home!
Quick!"

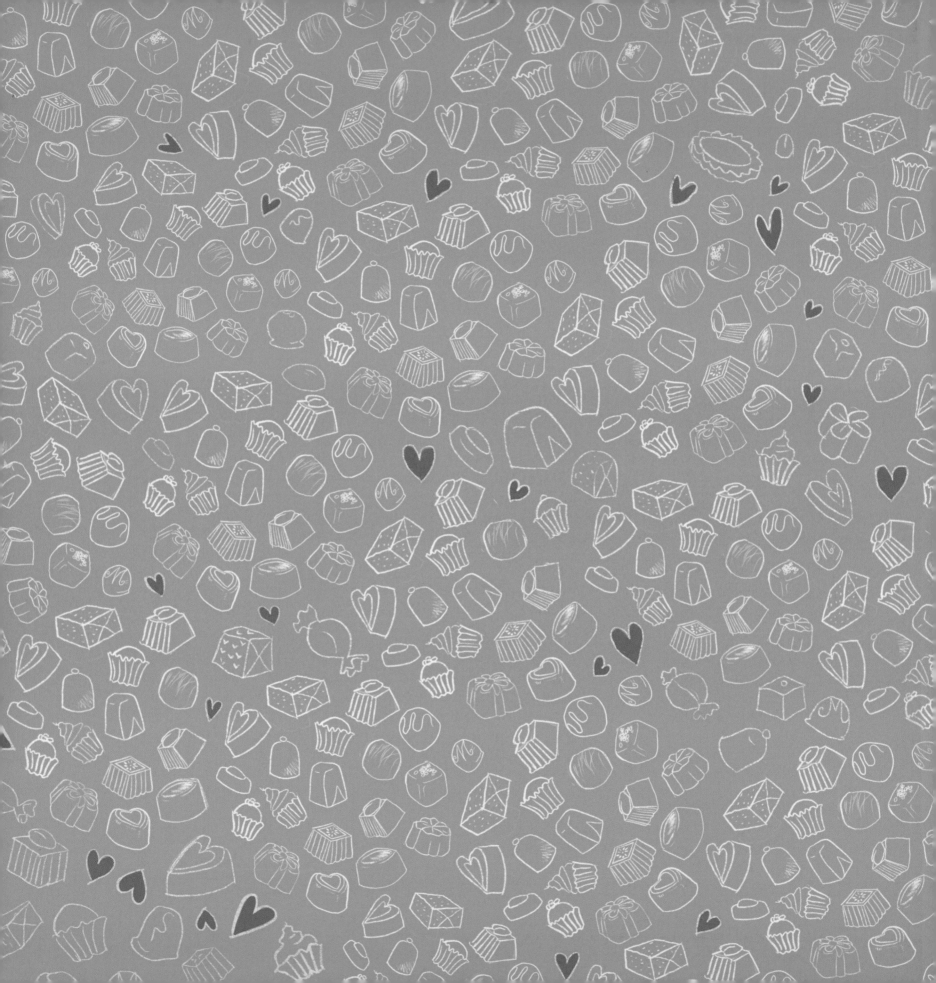